W9-CST-652

Cecilia Minden-Cupp, Ph.D.
Reading Specialist

by Bob Woods

Gareth Stevens Publishing
A WORLD ALMANAC EDUCATION GROUP COMPANY

Please visit our web site at: www.garethstevens.com
For a free color catalog describing Gareth Stevens Publishing's
list of high-quality books and multimedia programs,
call 1-800-542-2595 (USA) or 1-800-387-3178 (Canada).
Gareth Stevens Publishing's fax: (414) 332-3567.

Library of Congress Cataloging-in-Publication Data

Woods, Bob.
     Water sports / by Bob Woods.
          p. cm. — (Extreme sports: an imagination library series)
     Summary: Briefly describes new versions of surfing and water skiing, as well as newer
water sports such as kitesurfing and wakeboarding.
     Includes bibliographical references and index.
     ISBN 0-8368-3727-4 (lib. bdg.)
     1. Aquatic sports—Juvenile literature. [1. Aquatic sports.] I. Title. II. Extreme sports
(Milwaukee, Wis.)
GV770.5.W66   2003
797—dc21   2003042801

First published in 2004 by
Gareth Stevens Publishing
A World Almanac Education Group Company
330 West Olive Street, Suite 100
Milwaukee, WI 53212 USA

Text: Bob Woods
Cover design and page layout: Tammy Gruenewald
Series editor: Carol Ryback
Manuscript and photo research: Shoreline Publishing Group LLC

Photo credits: Cover © AP/Wide World Photos; p. 5 Ian Lauder; p. 7 Brian Nevins;
p. 9 Ralph Clevenger; p. 11 © Mark A. Johnson/CORBIS; p. 13 © Rick Doyle/CORBIS;
p. 15 © Sports Gallery/Al Messerschmidt; p. 17 © Art Underground/CORBIS; p. 19
© Joel W. Rogers/CORBIS; p. 21 © Tony Arruza/CORBIS

Printed in the United States of America

1 2 3 4 5 6 7 8 9 07 06 05 04 03

Cover: Water skiing on a **slalom ski**
requires an extreme sense of balance.

TABLE OF CONTENTS

Words that appear in the glossary are printed in **boldface** type the first time they occur in the text.

WET & WILD

Welcome to the wild world of water sports, where even water skiing has gotten extreme!

Fly off jumps on regular water skis or on a single slalom ski — or with no skis at all! Turn up the thrills by **kiteboarding** or **wakeboarding**. And don't forget about **windsurfing** through calm seas or skimming across mondo (totally awesome) waves.

Of course, **hanging ten** on a surfboard is still totally cool. You could also slip into a **kayak** and shoot some river **rapids** or ride the ocean waves.

Read on for more about the wild life on the water!

Sit down and let the speed of the boat pull you up and out of the water in an **air-chair hydrofoil water ski**.

SURF'S UP!

Surfing may be the world's oldest extreme sport. Over two hundred years ago, English explorers found Hawaiian Island natives riding the waves on huge wooden surfboards!

Hawaii is still a major surfer's paradise. Other surfing hot spots are in California, Australia, and South Africa.

Here's how to catch a wave: Lie on the surfboard and paddle past the **breakers**. Turn toward shore, sit up, and wait. Just before the wave breaks, start paddling. Angle the surfboard away from the **curl** of the wave. As you gain speed, stand up.

You're surfin', dude!

Sometimes expert surfers "shoot the tube" and literally ride inside the curl of a huge wave for a long glide. Most surfers strap a leash from their board to their ankle so they won't lose the board in case they fall — or "eat it."

WHEN THE WIND BLOWS . . .

In the late 1960s, somebody attached a sail to a surfboard and **sailboarding** — commonly known as windsurfing — was born. Windsurfing became so popular that it is now an Olympic sport.

Two basic types of windsurfing are light wind, for beginners, and high wind, for more experienced sailors. Very high winds and really big waves turn windsurfing into **wavesailing**, a most extreme sport.

Windsurfing boards have footstraps to keep your feet on the board. Beginners learn on longer boards for more steadiness. Extreme windsurfers use shorter boards for doing tricks more easily.

The first step in windsurfing is learning how to stand up and pull the sail up out of the water. As you start moving, keep your balance by pulling on the boom (the horizontal handle on the sail) while shifting your body weight.

GO FLY A KITE(BOARD)!

Kiteboarding is such an extreme sport that experts recommend lessons for everyone. In fact, the major skill of kiteboarding is learning to properly control the kite.

Launch the kite into the wind to start your ride. The kite has a frame and long lines that attach to a harness worn around your waist and hips. Strong winds give you more speed as they pull the kiteboard along the surface of the water.

A kiteboard has footstraps that help you control it during your flips, spins, and jumps. Always wear a life jacket when kiteboarding!

This experienced kitesurfer is heading out to the breakers. Out there he'll be able to do flips, turns, jumps, spins, and other tricks.

THE SCOOP ON WATER SKIING

Want to join the eleven million people in the United States who already know how to water ski? Just grab your life jacket, a helmet, and a pair of water skis, and find a fast boat with a tow rope.

Hop into the water behind the boat, slip your feet into the skis, and grab the rope. Put the rope between your skis. When the rope is pulled taut (tight) behind the boat, yell "Hit it!" to the driver — then hang on!

As the boat picks up speed, it will pull you up and out of the water. You're water skiing!

A slalom skier creates a huge rooster-tail **wake** as he leans toward the water. Awesome!

WIDE A-WAKEBOARDING

Wakeboarding is one of the fastest-growing water sports in the world. It's like skateboarding on water — only more extreme.

A wakeboarder gets towed behind a special boat that creates a bigger, wider wake than a regular ski boat. Special bindings keep your feet attached to the wakeboard. You catch air using the boat's wake as a takeoff ramp doing for jumps, flips, grabs, and other tricks.

Wakeboards come in an extreme variety of totally cool colors and outrageous designs.

Wakeboard competitions are very popular. Athletes compete in one of four categories: beginner, intermediate, advanced, and expert.

SHOOTIN' THE RAPIDS

Arctic peoples first used kayaks centuries ago for fishing and hunting. Kayaking as a sport began more than 150 years ago. In 1936, it became an official Olympic event.

A kayak's shape and size varies for different uses, number of riders, and water conditions. Touring kayaks are long and sleek to cut through ocean waves. Freestyle kayakers do tricks with their boats.

Extreme athletes "shoot the rapids" in kayaks designed to move easily through very fast, narrow, and usually very rocky areas where the river water is so wild it looks white.

Solo kayaks hold one person. Tandem kayaks hold two people.

An extreme kayaker must learn to handle the boat in many different water conditions, such as the wild and dangerous whitewater areas.

SEA KAYAKING

You can take an extreme trip in a sea kayak! Special storage holds carry food and equipment, so you can travel great distances across freshwater lakes or along an ocean coast for days on end.

Some extreme sea kayakers even surf the gnarly ocean waves or do tricks with their boats!

Kayakers use a special paddle with a blade on each end to control forward, backward, and sideways movements. If you don't know how to handle a kayak, you need to take lessons.

Make sure you wear a life jacket when kayaking.

Extreme sea kayakers ride the breaking waves as they surf, squirt (get the kayak up and keep it standing on its tail), or do other tricks.

THE JET SET

You often see people riding jet skis on rivers and lakes and near ocean coastlines. A jet ski is somewhat like a floating snowmobile. It has an accelerator and brakes.

Some people complain that jet skis are noisy and dangerous. But when operated responsibly, jet skis are fast, furious — and extreme fun!

Remember to wear your life jacket and obey the speed limit, or you could get a ticket.

Jet-ski racing is becoming a popular sport. Some jet-ski racers go faster than 70 mph (113 kph). Racers wear helmets for protection.

These girls are having a blast on a two-person jet ski. It's important to obey safety rules and watch out for other jet skiers and boaters.

MORE TO READ AND VIEW

Books (Nonfiction)   *Extreme Wakeboarding. Extreme Sports* (series).
   Anne T. McKenna (Capstone)
Freestyle Water Skiing. Action Sports Library (series).
   Bob Italia (ABDO)
In Water. Safety (series). Kyle Carter (Rourke)
Jet Skiing. Action Sports Library (series).
   Bob Italia and Rosemary Wallner (editor) (ABDO)
Kayaking. All Action (series). Alan Fox (Lerner)
Surfing. Extreme Sports (series). Chuck Miller (Raintree)
Windsurfing. Radical Sports (series).
   Amanda Barker (Heinemann)

Books (Fiction)   *Hawaiian Beach Party. You're Invited to Mary Kate and Ashley's*
   (series). Nancy Krulik (Scholastic)
Stranding on Cedar Point. Neptune Adventures, Vol. 4 (series).
   Susan Saunders (Camelot)
Surf's Up! Xocket Power Adventures, 2 (series).
   Terry Collins (Simon)

Videos (Nonfiction)   *Beginning Boardsailing.* (Bennett Media)
Beginning & Intermediate Water Skiing for Kids.
   (Derek Packard)
Liquid Stage: The Lure of Surfing. (Michael Bovee)
Performance Sea Kayaking. (John C. Davis)
Surfing for Life. (David L. Brown)
Trailside: Sea Kayaking Australia's Great Barrier Reef.
   (ABC Home Video)

22

WEB SITES

Web sites change frequently, but we believe the following web sites are going to last. You can also use good search engines, such as **Yahooligans! (www.yahooligans.com)** or **Google (www.google.com)** to find our more about water sports. Some keywords that will help you are: *aquatic sports, boat safety, jet skiing, kiteboarding, life jackets, sea kayaking, surfing, wakeboarding, water safety, water skiing, and windsurfing.*

www.kidscamps.com/sports/water_sport.html
KidsCamps.com includes information on water sports camps in your area.

www.surflifeforwomen.com/2002/ articles/rochellecamp.php
Read about the real-life adventure of a young female surfer as she shares the waves and a surfboard with a champion surfer.

www.onr.navy.mil/focus/ocean/ motion/waves2.htm
Learn about the science of a breaking wave on the shoreline. Easy-to-understand graphics highlight surging breakers, plunging breakers, and spilling breakers.

www.bam.gov/whiz_kids/expert/ water_skiing.htm
Bam! features an interview with water skiing champ Danyelle Bennett, as well as water skiing tips, safety information, and a link to USA Water Ski, a national association that regulates this extreme sport.

www.gokayak.com
Includes information on equipment, best kayaking locations, and lessons. Specializes in teaching beginners and others kayaking safety, how to "read" the water, and proper paddling techniques for water conditions.

www.boatsafe.com/kids/
Boat Safe Kids features boating safety tips, a special game of life-jacket tic-tac-toe, and questions and answers about boats and water safety from kids like you!

www.kiteboarding mag.com/
Kiteboarding magazine's web site provides information on the latest kiteboarding news, videos, and learning tips. Direct links allow viewers to read about kitesurfing celebrities and to watch them in action. Travel to the best kitesurfing locations, see the hottest gear, and check out the newest moves by current riders.

GLOSSARY

You can find these words on the pages listed. Reading a word in a sentence helps you understand it even better.

air-chair hydrofoil water ski — a type of water ski that rises up and out of the water and has a "chair" for the rider to sit upon. 4

breakers — waves near the shore that curl over and fall apart into foam. 6, 10

curl — a hollow arch or even a tube formed by breaking waves. "Shooting the tube" means riding inside the curl of the wave. 6

hanging ten — hanging all ten toes over the front edge of a surfboard. 4

kayak — a long, narrow boat that is pointed at both ends. 4, 16, 18

kiteboarding — kite-powered surfing. 4, 10

rapids — narrow and often rocky river areas with wild, fast-moving, foamy water. 4, 16

slalom ski — a single water ski that has footstraps for both feet. 2, 4, 12

wake — waves of water that form in the path of or shoot into the air behind a moving boat or body. 12, 14

wakeboarding — riding a board that is being towed in the wake of a boat. 4, 14

wavesailing — windsurfing in high winds and big waves. 8

windsurfing (sailboarding) — riding a surfboard that's fitted with a sail. 4, 8

INDEX